DR. JO

HOW SARA JOSEPHINE BAKER
SAVED THE LIVES OF AMERICA'S CHILDREN

MONICA KULLING

ILLUSTRATED BY
JULIANNA SWANEY

tundra

People called Sara Josephine Baker a tomboy. Jo did things that the quiet and polite girls of her day did not do. She played baseball. She climbed trees. She was strong and adventurous.

Jo was born in 1873 in Poughkeepsie, New York, a city on the banks of the Hudson River. She and her younger brother, Robbie, fished the river in summer and skated on it in winter.

The river was also a source of drinking water. But one year, when Jo was sixteen, tragedy struck. A hospital dumped its sewage in the river, which caused a typhoid fever epidemic.

Jo was heartbroken when Robbie died from typhoid. Three months later, Jo's father died from the same disease.

Jo had wanted to be a doctor ever since she was
ten years old, when a kind physician and his son, also a
doctor, had taken care of her injured knee. The deaths
of her father and brother renewed that dream.

In Jo's day, most people thought that studying medicine
was not for women.
"It's too grisly!" said some.
"It's too gruesome!" said others.

But a few women doctors were proving that this thinking was simple prejudice. In 1868, two doctors who were sisters — Emily and Elizabeth Blackwell — had founded the Women's Medical College of the New York Infirmary.

After high school, Jo applied to their school and was accepted! She boarded a train bound for New York City.

When Jo graduated in 1898, she and her friend Florence, who was also a doctor, set up a private practice together.

They hung out a sign and proudly let people know they were open for business.

Lillian Russell, a famous actress, was one of Dr. Jo's patients. She told her friends about the wonderful care she was getting from Dr. Baker.

Even with this help, Dr. Jo did not have enough patients to keep her in business. So, in 1901, she became a health inspector for the city of New York.

Dr. Jo was sent to a tough west-side neighborhood called Hell's Kitchen. Here, thousands of people, many of them immigrants, lived in run-down apartments. Diseases such as smallpox and typhoid fever spread like wildfire, especially among the young.

Dr. Jo was saddened to think of the many children who died there every week. She was determined to help.

Each morning Dr. Jo put on her sturdy walking shoes, picked up her medical bag and headed for Hell's Kitchen.

She was making her way to work one morning when a frantic man stopped her.

"Please come quick!" he said. "My baby is dying!"

Dr. Jo entered a gloomy room. When she saw three hungry children staring at her, she brought out her lunch. She split a hunk of cornbread into three parts.

The screaming baby was tightly wrapped in a blanket. Many mothers believed that this practice, called swaddling, kept newborns quiet. But summer's severe heat could be deadly.

As Dr. Jo unwound the blanket, she said, "This is not good."

And it wasn't. This baby, like many others, would die of heatstroke.

In the same building, Dr. Jo examined another baby with eye problems. The retinoscope shone a light into the retina, or back of the eye, to see if the eye was working.

"I'm so sorry," said Dr. Jo, sadly.

Silver nitrate drops used to clean bacteria from a newborn's eyes had instead made this baby blind.

Dr. Jo shared the stories of her day with Dr. Florence. While her friend listened, Jo ticked off the things every newborn needed.

"The eye drops must be an exact measure. Too often the solution evaporates or the glass container is dirty. The result? Damaged eyes.

"Newborns also need clothes that let them move. They need fresh air and clean milk. Children need a safe place to play, not streets that are filled with garbage and manure! In short, Hell's Kitchen has earned its name!"

Jo did her best thinking while walking. On a rare day off, she walked to the bottom of Manhattan Island. She looked out at the statue that welcomed newcomers from other countries.

Jo was seeing firsthand how grateful immigrants were to live in America, but also how hard that new life could be if you were poor.

Dr. Jo desperately wanted to help, and she had a few ideas.

She began by looking at the practice of home births, which were common among immigrant women. Midwives helped with the birthing process, but many of these women did not know what to do if something went wrong. Dr. Jo made it a requirement for midwives to take courses to earn a license. She sent nurses to help new mothers in their first days at home with their babies.

Dr. Jo also organized milk stations in storefronts throughout the city so that mothers could get clean, healthy milk for their children.

Then Jo put her mind to the problem of the flawed eye-drop containers. One day, while sitting in Bowling Green Park, she watched bees at work. Jo knew that beeswax was antibacterial, antifungal, antiseptic and even antiviral. It was everything the doctor ordered!

Beeswax made the perfect eye-drop container. The midwife could be confident that the drops were clean and perfectly measured. And mothers could rest easy too.

Dr. Jo tackled another problem — swaddling — by designing her own infant wear. Her sleeper opened down the front. It made changing diapers easier and allowed for movement and better temperature control.

A pattern company bought Dr. Jo's sleeper and mass-produced it. Soon mothers were making safer baby clothes.

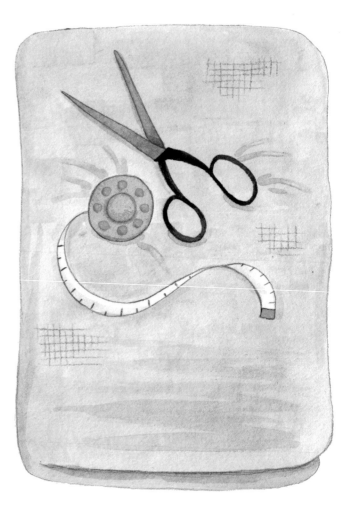

Dr. Jo understood the connection between poverty
and illness. Throughout her life she worked tirelessly
to improve the health of women and their children in
New York and other big cities.

By the end of her career, Dr. Sara Josephine Baker had
saved the lives of 90,000 inner-city children across America.
People were always happy to see Dr. Jo coming their way!

More about Dr. Jo

In 1908, when Dr. Sara Josephine Baker became the first director of the New York City Department of Child Hygiene, she also became its first pediatrician (pee-dee-uh-TRISH-uhn). A pediatrician is a doctor who is trained to diagnose and treat child illnesses.

Dr. Jo's many health-care ideas broke new ground. One of her practical ideas was called the Little Mothers' League. Girls age 12 and older were trained in basic infant care, such as feeding a baby, care of milk in the home and what to do if a baby is teething. When older children were able to care for their younger brothers and sisters, both parents could work to increase the household's finances.

For much of her career, Dr. Jo worked in Hell's Kitchen, now called Clinton. No one knows the exact origin of the name Hell's Kitchen, but the west-side area was littered with menacing nicknames like Battle Row and the House of Blazes (where setting fires was a favorite pastime). Hell's Kitchen was known for its violence.

Wherever the name came from, it was brave Dr. Jo who took on the job of helping those who needed her help the most — infants and children. By the time she retired in 1923, New York City had the lowest infant mortality rate of any major American city.

SOURCES

BOOKS

Baker, S. Josephine. *Fighting for Life*. New York: Macmillan, 1939.

Ptacek, Greg. *Champion for Children's Health: A Story about Dr. S. Josephine Baker*. Minneapolis: Carolrhoda Books, 1994.

WEBSITES

https://cfmedicine.nlm.nih.gov/physicians/biography_19.html

https://www.ncbi.nlm.nih.gov/pmc/articles/PMC1470556/

https://www.britannica.com/biography/Sara-Josephine-Baker

For Barbara and Nancy, doctors' daughters, and for
Dr. Cheryl, in gratitude — MK

For Mom, Dad and Aradan — JS

Tundra Books, an imprint of Penguin Random House Canada Young Readers,
a Penguin Random House Company

Library and Archives Canada Cataloguing in Publication

Kulling, Monica, 1952–, author
      Dr. Jo / by Monica Kulling ; illustrated by Julianna Swaney.
Issued in print and electronic formats.
ISBN 978-1-101-91789-3 (hardcover).—ISBN 978-1-101-91791-6 (EPUB)

1. Baker, S. Josephine (Sara Josephine), 1873–1945—Juvenile literature. 2.
Health officers—New York (State)—New York—Biography—Juvenile literature.
I. Swaney, Julianna, illustrator II. Title.

RA424.5.B33K84 2018   j610.92 C2017-905564-X
                                                    C2017-905565-8

Published simultaneously in the United States of America by Tundra Books
of Northern New York, an imprint of Penguin Random House Canada Young
Readers, a Penguin Random House Company

Library of Congress Control Number: 2017951210

Edited by Jessica Burgess and Elizabeth Kribs
Designed by Leah Springate
The artwork in this book was created with watercolor, gouache and colored pencil.
The text was set in Bembo Book.

Printed and bound in China

www.penguinrandomhouse.ca

1 2 3 4 5   22 21 20 19 18

Penguin
Random House
tundra | TUNDRA BOOKS